Mummy and Me

This book belongs to:

_____

This edition published by Parragon Books Ltd in 2018

Parragon Books Ltd
Chartist House
15–17 Trim Street
Bath BA1 1HA, UK
www.parragon.com

Written by Tiya Hall
Illustrated by Sydney Hanson
Edited by Lily Holland
Designed by Kathryn Davies
Production by Michaela Bartzsch

ISBN 978-1-4748-9229-2

Printed in China

Mummy
and Me

PaRRagon

Bath • New York • Cologne • Melbourne • Delhi
Hong Kong • Shenzhen • Singapore

The sky is blue, the sun is bright,
I'm **happy** as can be.
I'm ready for a day of fun...
Just my **mum** and **me**!

We **paddle** in the river,

We **splash** about and swim,

And if I'm feeling very brave...

We do a big jump in!

If I can't see what's ahead
Or if I'm feeling small,

She lifts me on her shoulder
So that I feel big and tall.

We **hide** and
seek together,

And we
jump about
and play,

We **roll** around and **giggle**,
We love playing games all day.

We spend our days
exploring,

And building
secret dens,

Having new adventures,
And making **lots** of **friends**.

And if I'm feeling funny,
Or a little bit **unsure**,

She finds a way to help,
So I'm not worried any more!

It's true I sometimes make **mistakes,**

But mummy doesn't mind.